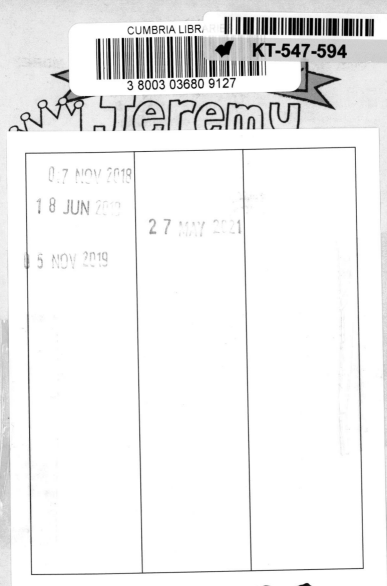

PUFFIN

PUFFIN BOOKS

UK | USA | Canada | Ireland | Australia
India | New Zealand | South Africa

Puffin Books is part of the Penguin Random House group of companies
whose addresses can be found at global.penguinrandomhouse.com.

puffinbooks.com

Penguin
Random House
UK

First published 2015
001

Text copyright © Jeremy Strong, 2015
Illustrations copyright © Rowan Clifford, 2015

The moral right of the author and illustrator has been asserted

Set in Baskerville MT
Printed in Great Britain by Clays Ltd, St Ives plc

A CIP catalogue record for this book is available from the British Library

ISBN: 978-0-141-35772-0

This is for Peter Scott, whose help at a crucial moment during the birth of this story was received with thanks and enormous relief.

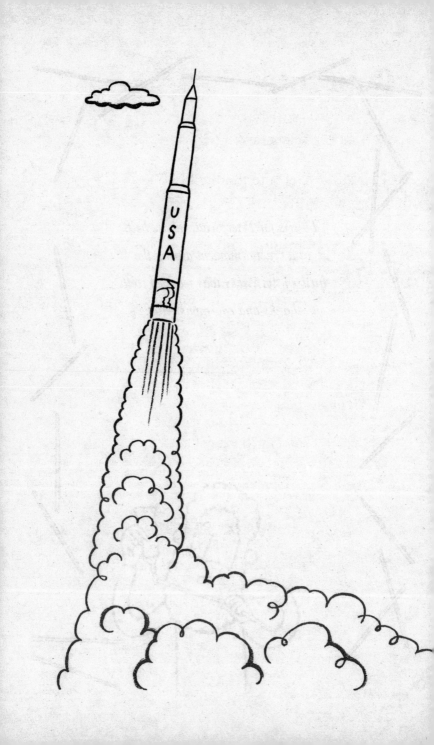

Contents

1. Finders Keepers

My dad came home with a sheep yesterday. He says it followed him. 'I was on my way home and there was this sheep standing in the road.'

Mum was unimpressed. 'Sheep don't just follow you,' she told him.

'This one did,' said Dad. 'I think it was because I said hello.'

'That's ridiculous.' Mum turned to me. 'Have you ever heard of a sheep following anyone, Nicholas?'

'Er, Little Bo Peep?' I suggested.

'That's a nursery rhyme,' Mum pointed out.

'Little Bo Peep went beep beep beep!' shouted Cheese. Mum and Dad both ignored him.

'BEEP BEEP BEEP!' echoed Tomato before bursting into giggles. Mum and Dad ignored her too. (In case you're wondering why the twins are called Cheese and Tomato, it's because they were born in the back of a pizza van. It was Dad's idea, of course. But that's *another* story!)

'Look,' said Dad, 'I didn't ask the sheep to follow me. He just did. His name is Elvis.'

'Dad! How do you know that?' I asked.

'Just look at him, Nicholas. Doesn't he look like an Elvis to you?'

The sheep was trying to eat Cheese's slipper, which was lying in the middle of the floor. The other one was probably out in the garden or up a tree, anywhere except where it should be – on Cheese's left foot. Anyhow, I thought he looked more like a Darren.

Mum heaved a very large sigh. 'He'll have to go in the garden,' she said, scowling at Dad.

'Well, I wasn't thinking of putting him in our bedroom,' he grunted.

'Ron, what you are thinking is often a complete mystery to me AND the rest of the world.'

They stared at each other until Dad gave a big grin and burst into song:

'*You are the love of my life. And you are the reason I'm alive . . .*'

'Stop it!' laughed Mum. 'You're such a clown!' She began pushing him out of the house, along with the sheep.

So it looked like Elvis was here to stay, at least for a while.

'He must belong to someone,' Mum said as she came back in. 'Sheep don't just hang around on street corners, waiting to follow some turnip home.'

'I heard that!' Dad called from the garden. 'I'm not a turnip. Do I look like a turnip, Nicholas?'

I eyed Dad carefully. 'If that sheep can be an Elvis then I reckon you could just about be a turnip, Dad.'

'Well, thank you very much,' Dad grunted. 'After all the things I've done for you. I changed your nappy when you were a baby —'

'No you didn't,' Mum broke in. 'You said you couldn't hold your nose and change a

nappy at the same time.'

'OK, but what about all those other things I did? I cooked his supper —'

Mum shook her head. 'No, Ron, you *tried* to cook Nicholas's supper, but you burnt it, remember? In fact, you set light to a tea towel.'

'I didn't do it on purpose. Anyhow, what else have I done for you, Nicholas? I taught you how to blow raspberries. There! I was very good at that.'

'I know, Dad, and when I went to school the next day we had Show and Tell and I showed and told everyone in class how to blow raspberries and I was sent to the headteacher for being rude.'

Dad held up his hands in despair. 'OK, I surrender. I haven't done anything at all for you.'

I smiled. 'It's all right, Dad. I don't mind. You're the best dad in the world. I bet there aren't many dads who bring home sheep.'

'Or alligators,' added Mum. 'Don't forget Crunchbag the alligator.'

'Exactly,' said Dad, suddenly perking up. 'You're right, Nicholas. There can't be many dads like me!' And he grinned broadly at all of us. 'I should be in the *Big Book of World Records* for being the, er, somethingest dad in the world.'

'Strangest?' suggested Mum, and Dad made a face at her.

'Silly Daddy!' shouted Tomato.

'That's it exactly,' agreed Mum. 'The SILLIEST dad in the world. That fits perfectly.'

'Thank you very much,' said Dad, giving us a bow.

So that was that. We now have a sheep in the garden. We also have five chickens (that's Captain Birdseye, Mavis Moppet, Beaky and Leaky and Poop), two rabbits, Rubbish the goat and Schumacher the tortoise. Mum says that Elvis must belong to someone so she's going to ring all the local farmers and find out if anyone is missing a sheep.

'Meanwhile, I suppose he will have to stay with us,' she said. 'I hope Mr Tugg won't mind.'

Mr Tugg is our neighbour. If you haven't met him yet I had better warn you. Imagine a hurricane mixed with a volcano and then throw in some bits of earthquake, an avalanche and a couple of tsunamis – that's what Mr Tugg is like. He is a bumper collection of natural disasters all squeezed into one small, bald-headed, exploding human. (Although my dad says that Mr Tugg is really a Martian alien from outer space.)

Elvis the sheep soon made friends with Rubbish. They followed each other round the garden and at night they slept together, with Elvis resting his head on the goat's fat belly. It

was very sweet. Dad said that maybe they should get married and then we could call them Mr and Mrs Sheegoat. Or Mr and Mrs Gosheep. Mr and Mrs Rubbish perhaps?

It was a whole day before Mr Tugg realized we had a sheep living with us and when he did he wasn't very impressed. He stood at the fence, staring with bulging eyes.

'Is that what I think it is?' he snapped.

Dad leaped back as if he'd just had a terrible fright. 'Argh! The Martians have arrived! Run for your lives!'

'Very funny,' scowled Mr Tugg. 'I said, is that what I think it is?'

'I don't know,' Dad replied. 'What do you think it is?'

'A sheep, of course!'

'Then of course it's a sheep,' Dad answered calmly. 'Well spotted. I hereby award you a first-class sheep-spotter's badge. You can sew it on your scout jumper.'

Mr Tugg's face began to change colour. 'Are you allowed to keep sheep in your back garden in a residential area? Do you have a permit? I shall check with the local council.'

'Really, Mr Tugg? Must you check everything? Do you have a permit?'

'What are you talking about? What do I need a permit for?'

'Breathing,' Dad shot back. 'Do you have permission from the council to breathe? Because if you don't you'll just have to pack it in, you know.'

'Will you ever stop talking nonsense?' growled Mr Tugg. He was getting redder by the second, which was a big Danger Signal. Any moment now he would blow his top and we'd have a Major Explosion on our hands and the prime minister would have to declare our road a Disaster Area.

Fortunately, just at that moment, Mrs Tugg appeared. I like Mrs Tugg. She is round and wobbly and jolly. She looked over the fence and spotted Elvis at once.

'What a lovely sheep!' she declared.

Mr Tugg looked at his wife in surprise.

'Isn't it pretty?' she went on.

'Pretty? It's a sheep,' Mr Tugg pointed out.

'Yes, dear, and a rather funky one. It looks like an Elvis to me.'

'Mrs Tugg, you are a wonder!' cried Dad. 'Will you marry me?'

Mr Tugg snorted. 'Don't be ridiculous.'

But Mrs Tugg was shaking with laughter.

'That's amazing!' Dad continued. 'See, Nicholas? I told you his name was Elvis.'

I just grinned at everyone.

'You can't call a sheep Elvis,' Mr Tugg grunted.

'Oh? Do I need a permit for that too?' asked Dad.

'Stop being such a killjoy, dear,' Mrs Tugg said, and she gave Mr Tugg a playful tweak of his ear.

'Ow!' He leaped back from the fence. 'I'm

going indoors to ring the council,' he said. 'What's more, I would like to know where you got that sheep from. It didn't come from any pet shop that I know of. They don't sell sheep.'

'It followed me home,' said Dad. 'Finders keepers.'

'Pish!' snapped Mr Tugg and, turning on his heel, he marched into his house.

Mrs Tugg looked at my dad and shook her head.

'Oh dear,' she sympathized. 'You know what my husband's like. I'm afraid we haven't heard the last of this.'

'No,' agreed Dad. 'We probably haven't.' He turned to the sheep. 'You hear that, Elvis? You'd better go into hiding. Mr Tugg is after your fleece.'

2. How to Get Into the Big Book of World Records

'The thing is,' Dad told Mum later, 'sheep are very useful creatures.'

'Really? Are you saying that because you don't have to mow the lawn now that Elvis is happily mowing it for you, with his teeth?'

'No I'm not. Don't be so cynical. It's not becoming. Cynical people end up with mouths that are twisted downwards and narrow, slitty eyes, not to mention narrow minds.'

Mum laughed. 'Go on then, tell me why sheep are so useful.'

'One: you can collect their wool. Two: you can spin their wool. Three: you can knit jumpers and jackets and blankets and bobble hats with their wool, not to mention hot-water-bottle covers.

In fact, you could kit out the whole family with woolly clothes.'

Mum thought for a moment. 'I've got a better idea. One: YOU could collect the wool. Two: YOU could spin it. And three: YOU could do all the knitting. How about that?'

'I'm too busy,' said Dad, relaxing back in his armchair and pretending to smoke an imaginary pipe. 'You see, what you have to understand is that I'm an Ideas Man, a Creative Person. I'm a Thinker.'

'Daddy's a stinker!' cried Cheese, poking his head out from behind Dad's chair.

'I didn't say that, you rat!' shouted Dad, trying to reach behind to grab Cheese, who was far too quick and already by the door, poised to make his escape.

'Stinky Daddy! POO!' he yelled before racing upstairs, giggling his head off.

'I don't know why you brought up our children to be so rude to their father,' Dad complained, his face the picture of innocence.

'ME!?' cried Mum. 'Who taught them how to blow raspberries? Who taught them silly nonsense words?'

Dad simply carried on puffing at his non-existent pipe. 'Anyway,' he continued eventually, 'as I said earlier, I'm a Thinker and as such I have been thinking. It's something that came to me when you said I should be in the *Big Book of World Records*.'

'Actually, Dad, *you* said that, not any of us,' I pointed out.

'Really? *I* said it? Doesn't that just show what a brainbox I am? I said something even before I'd thought of it. It's like being awake before you've even woken up. Anyway, as I was saying, I should be in the *Big Book of World Records* so that is exactly what I am going to do. I am going to be a record-breaker.'

'Really? Wow!' I was impressed. My dad was going to get into the *Big Book of World Records*! But what record was he going to break? I had to ask him.

'I'm not sure, Nicholas. It's something I shall have to think about very hard.'

At that moment Cheese came zooming back into the room like an escaped balloon with all the air rushing out of it. He hurled himself on to Dad's lap, shouted 'Stinky-poo!' and then he was off again, leaving Dad completely winded.

'Sometimes,' muttered Dad, slowly getting his breath back, 'I think I should have a world record for being The Dad Who Has Survived the Most Attacks from Three-year-old Toddlers.'

Luckily, Dad was saved from any more toddler terrorists by Granny and Lancelot. As Dad let them in at the front door, Mum whispered to me that she thought it was interesting how often Granny and Lancelot turned up at mealtimes.

'It's nearly always just before lunch or supper,' she murmured, giving me a wink.

Granny and Lancelot are great. Granny's first husband died and a few years later she met Lancelot. He's got a ponytail and a leather jacket with fringes on the arms and the most massive motorbike, with a sidecar. Sometimes Granny rides it. She used to be a motorbike champion when she was young. Guess where Granny and Lancelot got married? On a bouncy castle! How cool is that?!

'Hello, Nicholas,' said Gran. 'Have you got a kiss for your old granny?'

'Hey, babe, less of the old,' said Lancelot. 'I've got a kiss for you any time!'

I looked at Cheese and Tomato, who were watching with their mouths open in horror. I called to them: 'One, two, three –'

And we all shouted, '*YURRRKKKK!!!!*' Then the twins ran away to hide because they were afraid Lancelot would chase them, which is what he usually does.

Granny smiled and waved a dismissive hand at me. 'Oh well, ignore your poor old granny. Now what's for supper? Smells like spaghetti to me.'

'It *is* spaghetti,' said Mum. 'But I'm afraid there's only enough for six, and there'll be seven of us if you two stay.' She gave me another wink.

'That's all right,' said Gran. 'Cheese and Tomato can share. They are a bit on the podgy side, aren't they? They could do with a bit less to eat.'

'Granny! The twins aren't podgy at all,' I told her.

'I didn't say they were stodgy,' complained Gran. 'I said podgy.'

Sometimes Granny doesn't hear things properly.

'I said podgy too,' I explained carefully.

'I never said stodgypoo,' Granny grumbled.

'Nobody said stodgypoo!' I tried not to shout.

'Stodgypoo!' shouted Cheese, who always picks up on words with 'poo' in them. He is only three.

'Excuse me,' said Dad, joining in. 'In fact, all three of you have said stodgypoo, and I just have too, so now four of us have said it.'

'WILL YOU ALL PLEASE STOP SAYING STODGYPOO OUT THERE?!' Mum yelled from the kitchen.

Dad pointed at his mother. 'You see what you've started?'

'Me?' Granny tried to look as innocent as possible, just as Mum came into the room with the food.

'I found enough for seven after all, so nobody will go hungry,' she announced.

Lancelot sniffed his plate of spaghetti and grinned up at Mum. 'You're a lifesaver!' he declared.

Granny shot him a look. 'She's a wife flavour? Are you suggesting this spaghetti has a wife flavour?'

'I SAID LIFESAVER, BABE!' Lancelot shouted back.

'Oh, you!' cried Granny, punching him playfully on the arm. She took a mouthful of spaghetti. 'You're always teasing me. Wife flavour! It doesn't taste like that at all.'

Lancelot rolled his eyes at me while Mum suggested that we ate our food without saying another word because if we didn't, she would probably run screaming from the room.

Tomato started to open her mouth to see if Mum really would run screaming from the room, but Mum stopped her in her tracks by lifting one finger of warning.

'DON'T – EVEN – THINK – ABOUT – IT!'
she said slowly and sternly.

So we sat there and ate our spaghetti in silence
for a while and then carefully we began to talk
again, glancing at Mum to see if she was going to
have the screaming abdabs or not. (She wasn't.)

Dad was looking at the few bits of spaghetti
left on his plate as if they were terribly important.
I thought at first that he'd discovered the
Meaning of Life in them, but no, he had hit
upon something much simpler. He lifted his head
from his plate and looked
round the table at all of us
in turn.

'I have an announcement to make,' he began. 'I am going to set a world record. It's something that nobody has ever tried to achieve before, something truly extraordinary and daring. It will place my name among the greatest record-breakers of all time.'

'What are you going to do, Dad?' I asked, bursting with excitement.

'I am going to create the longest single piece of spaghetti – *in the world*!'

Hmmmmm. The longest piece of spaghetti in the world? That didn't sound very exciting at all. Lancelot wasn't impressed either.

'Is that it?' he asked.

Dad smiled. 'You don't understand, Lancelot. My piece of spaghetti won't just be long. It will be $L - O - N - G$.'

Granny sighed and patted Mum's hand comfortingly. 'I'm afraid Ron never could stop playing with his food. I remember when he was a child I gave him egg and chips. Before I knew it, he'd turned the whole plate into a face with eggs for eyes, a sausage for a mouth and a big bit of bacon flopping over the sausage like a horrible, fat tongue poking out at me.'

Dad just sat there and grinned. Granny got up from her chair and laid a gentle hand on Mum's shoulder.

'Good luck, dear,' she said. 'Come on, my knight in shining armour, the food's all gone. Time we went home.'

3. Mum Falls Into a Hole

Dad's started on his record-breaking attempt! He's got a big packet of spaghetti and he's spread it all out on the dining table.

'Here's the plan,' he told me and the twins. 'I am going to stick one piece of spaghetti to another, end to end.'

'How?' I asked.

'With superglue! Ta-da!' Dad held up a tube of *FIXIT-FOREVER* – *the glue that sticks EVERYTHING* – *FOREVER!* (At least that's what it said on the side.)

'Superglue!' shouted Tomato.

'Superpoo!' shouted Cheese, even louder, and they both collapsed in hysterics.

Dad clamped a hand to his forehead. 'Won't you two ever stop? Why don't you go and play with your mother?'

'Mum's on the phone,' I told him. 'She's ringing all the local farmers to see if anyone's lost a sheep. But she did say she's taking the twins to see Granny and Lancelot when she's finished.'

Dad grunted and began arranging spaghetti all over the table. It was going to be a long business, especially as several bits of spaghetti were already stuck firmly to the table, but not to each other. I decided it would be wiser to let him get on with it, so I went out to the back garden to feed the animals.

I'd only been out there five minutes when Mum came out of the house.

'I got through to every farmer except one. I've tried him three times, but he never answers. None of the others have reported a missing sheep. I'll ring the last one again when I get back from Granny's. Will you be OK here with Dad?'

'Of course. It will take me a while to feed all this lot. See you later.'

Mum grabbed the twins, told Dad he'd *better-get-that-stuck-spaghetti-off-her-best-table-before-she-got-back-or-there'd-be-trouble* and off they went.

All went quiet, but not for long. There was a loud shout from inside the house. I turned to look and the first thing I noticed was that Mum had left the back door open. The second thing I noticed was that Elvis and Rubbish had vanished. My heart didn't just sink into my boots, it nosedived into my socks at supersonic speed and proceeded to burrow into the ground beneath.

THEY MUST BE IN THE HOUSE!

I raced back indoors. Disaster! Dad was on
his hands and knees in the hall, scrabbling about
madly in a forest of spaghetti, trying to stop
Rubbish and Elvis from wandering all over his
record-breaking attempt. Why on earth was he in
the hall? I had no idea and it wasn't the time to
ask either.

'GET THESE ANIMALS OUT OF HERE!'
Dad yelled.

I grabbed Rubbish by the collar and pulled the
complaining creature out into the garden. Then
I went back to get Elvis, who was sitting on a pile

of spaghetti, chewing several of the sticks. I got behind him and pushed and pushed until he went clattering off down the hall, through the kitchen and outside. I followed to make sure both animals were now safely secure in the garden.

There was another mighty roar from the house.

'NOOOOOOOOOOO!!!'

Then the doorbell rang.

BRRRRINNGGG!

'I'm coming!' Dad bellowed. 'Wait, I'm coming! Got a bit of a problem! With you in a minute, or two, or fifteen!'

BRRRRINNGGGG!!

'I said I'M COMING! Nicholas, help me! Help!'

I dashed back into the house and the craziest sight met my eyes. My dad was staggering round the hall, trying to open the front door, but he couldn't because both his hands were covered in spaghetti, sticking out at every angle. It looked like he had two giant, angry porcupines on the end of each arm instead of hands. He couldn't reach for anything without the spaghetti sticks getting in the way. Then I saw his feet were covered too – great mats of spaghetti were stuck to the soles of his shoes.

'Dad! What happened?!'

'I was trying to shoo those wretched animals away and I trod on the Fixit-Forever tube without realizing and squirted superglue all over the spaghetti. When I went to pick it up it just kept sticking to me and −'

BRRRRIINNNGGGGGG!!!

'I'll get it, Dad. Can you just move out of the way so I can squeeze past? Oh! I've got spaghetti stuck to my feet now!'

I managed to reach the front door and pulled it open. A smartly dressed woman was standing in the porch with one finger raised to the bell button as if she was about to ring yet again. She stared aghast as Dad lumbered towards her, slowly lifting his monster feet and waving his bristling spaghetti-hands at her.

'Hello?' said Dad, giving her a weak smile.

The woman's mouth fell open, but no sound came out and her eyes filled with terror. She turned tail and made a dash for safety, back up

the garden path, where she ran straight into
Mum and Cheese and Tomato.

'S-S-S-S-Save me!' she stuttered, pointing back
over her shoulder. She threw both arms
round my mother and
clutched her as if she
was some kind of
lifebelt.

Mum looked over the woman's shoulder
towards the house. She took a deep breath,
closed her eyes for a few moments and composed

herself. Then she peeled the woman's arms from their grip and held her by the shoulders.

'It's quite all right. You're perfectly safe. That's my husband.'

The woman's eyes widened. 'Your husband? You live with – that!?'

'Yes, I live with – THAT.'

'Daddy's a hedgepodge!' Cheese cried, jumping up and down and pointing.

'Hedgehog,' said Mum. 'And, Nicholas, you look a bit . . . hedgepodgy too. Don't tell me, your father had an accident with the superglue and now he's fixed forever to hundreds of spaghetti sticks.'

I nodded. 'But it wasn't his fault.'

'It's never his fault,' sighed Mum. 'So how did it happen?'

'Rubbish and Elvis got into the house and caused a bit of a problem.'

'And how did the animals manage to get inside?' asked Mum.

'Someone left the back door open.'

'And what idiot did that?' Mum demanded angrily.

'Well,' I began slowly, because I knew I was now treading on dangerous ground, 'you remember you came out to tell me you'd finished phoning the farmers and —'

I didn't need to finish. I could tell from Mum's face that she had just fallen into the hole she had dug for herself.

She closed her eyes again. Dad and I stood there like lemons — lemons encrusted with spaghetti sticks — and waited.

'I see,' Mum said at last. 'I think we'd better get cleared up, hadn't we? Now then,' she added, turning to the woman, who was still looking at all of us as if we were way beyond madness and had possibly come from a distant planet called Utterly Bonkers.

'Now then,' repeated Mum. 'How can we help you?'

4. To Infinity and Beyond!

'Are you sure it's safe?' the woman asked.

'Oh yes,' Mum answered breezily. 'My husband is trying to set a world record.'

'A world record?'

'Yes. He's trying to see if he can get more bits of spaghetti stuck to him than anyone else.'

'I didn't know there was a world record for that sort of thing,' said the woman, still eyeing Dad with alarm.

'No, neither did he, but now that he's got this far he may as well carry on. Shall we go inside? Do follow me. I think we need a cup of tea.'

Dad began making strange noises and waving his spaghetti fists at us. '*Wahhhhh –*'

The woman looked to Mum for enlightenment.

'He's trying to tell us that he can't drink tea

with his hands,' said Mum and she turned to Dad. 'Don't worry, you can have one of the twin's feeder beakers.'

Dad's face creased into a glare. 'You're enjoying my discomfort, aren't you?'

'You do look quite amusing, Ron,' Mum told him as she pottered about the kitchen.

When the tea was ready we went and sat at the dining-room table, crunching our way across the floor through the many strands of spaghetti still stuck to it.

'So what can we do for you?' Mum asked.

The woman took a big gulp of tea. 'It's about Cheese. He *is* called Cheese, isn't he?'

'His name is James,' said Mum, 'but my husband – this spaghetti-fied creature here – thought we should call him Cheese, and his sister Tomato, because they were both born in the back of a pizza-delivery van.'

'How very strange,' the woman said in a rather weak and wondering voice.

'Yes. I married a strange man, and I must admit that I knew he was strange when I married him. I just didn't know how strange – until today.' Mum went to pat Dad's hand and instead found herself patting several prickly sticks of snapped-off spaghetti. 'Ow!'

'As I was saying, I'm really here about Cheese – James. My name is Alisha. Do you know anything about the latest space rocket and the WhoTube competition?'

We all shook our heads.

'But you do know what WhoTube is?'

I nodded. I was always looking at it. 'It has loads of videos and stuff from around the world. Anyone can upload stuff they've done.'

'That's it,' agreed Alisha. 'Well, they have been running a competition along with NASA, the American space agency. The agency will soon be launching a special rocket and –'

'– they want to send Cheese into space!' added Dad, suddenly cheering up.

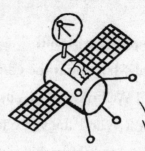

Alisha smiled. 'Do let me finish. Once the rocket is well beyond Earth's gravitational pull, a small detachable probe will separate from the rocket, its engines will be fired up and that probe will set off into deep space, on its way to unknown territory. It's designed to carry information to any other living beings – aliens – that might be out there in our universe. The probe will be packed with information about Earth and the humans who live on it.'

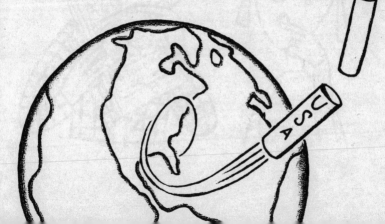

'Impressive,' I said.

'But what about the competition?' asked Dad.

'Ah! Well now, NASA asked people to vote on the best WhoTube video to send into outer space – something that would show what life on our planet Earth was all about.'

Alisha's face took on a strange appearance as she struggled to explain. 'Several people nominated Cheese and, believe it or not, the video of Cheese's bottom on the national news won the competition.'

Alisha looked utterly flabbergasted. So did my mum.

'You mean Cheese's bottom is going to show any alien beings out there in space that life on Earth is like a baby's bottom?'

Alisha gulped. 'Yes,' she croaked.

'Oh boy!' I could barely whisper. 'Oh boy, oh boy, oh boy!'

Dad grinned at us. 'I love democracy,' he declared bafflingly.

'So NASA *is* going to send Cheese into space!'

'Just the video – not Cheese himself,' Alisha pointed out.

'Oh, shame,' muttered Dad, and

Mum tried to poke him but got bitten by the
spaghetti again.

'Anyhow,' continued Alisha, 'because Cheese
has won such an amazing competition, I am here
to tell you that your family has been invited to go
and see the launch of the rocket itself.'

My eyes almost fell out. My brain was dancing.

'In America?' I gasped.

'In America, at the Kennedy Space Center.'

'OH WOW.' I could hardly breathe.

'The whole family?' asked Mum.

Alisha looked across the table at Dad, who was sitting there with his elbows resting on it because he had to keep his hands up in the air.

'All five of you,' said Alisha, 'although your husband might have to do something about the spaghetti. I don't think he'll be allowed into the USA like that.'

'I'm surprised he's allowed into this house,' muttered Mum and we all laughed, apart from Dad, who tried to appear above it all.

'You'll be away for almost a week,' Alisha told us. 'You'll have a couple of days in New York and then you fly down to Orlando, Florida, and the Kennedy Space Center.'

'New York!' I was so excited I wanted to scream.

'New forks!' shouted Cheese, who was just as excited as everyone else, but didn't really know why.

Alisha handed over a fat folder with all sorts of things inside – info about the Kennedy Space Center and our journey, hotel details, plane tickets and so on. She finished her tea, congratulated us all and left.

Mum went straight to the computer and set about finding out how to get rid of superglue. Then she got some nail-polish remover from the bathroom.

'Sit here,' she ordered Dad. 'Keep your hand still.' It took more than an hour, but eventually Mum managed to remove the glue and the spaghetti from one hand.

'There. Now you have one hand free, you can do the rest yourself. And don't forget to do your shoes as well. After that there's the table and the hall floor. And if I see you sticking any more spaghetti anywhere I shall – Fix YOU Forever!'

Dad grinned at her and began to sing. '*You are the sunshine of my life . . .*'

'No! Stop it!' laughed Mum, clapping her hands over her ears. 'I'm not listening!'

5. New York! New York!

We're on a plane! We're going to America! I can't believe it. New York! The Kennedy Space Center! We are sitting in Business Class, which means we get bigger seats that fold down so you can sleep on them and they give you a glass of champagne too. (Well, they give it to the adults. Children aren't allowed, of course. WE NEVER ARE! Adults always get the good stuff, as you well know.)

Cheese and Tomato spent the first half-hour

 making their seats fold flat and then go back up again and then go flat, endlessly.

Eventually, an air hostess came along and told them to sit up properly or the plane wouldn't take off.

'I want to see it flap its wings,' grumbled Cheese, who wasn't quite tall enough to see out of the window.

'Planes don't flap their wings,' I told him.

'How does it fly then?' he asked and Dad smirked at me.

'Yes, Nicholas,' said Dad. 'How *does* a plane fly? Please explain the laws of aerodynamics to Cheese and me. We REALLY, REALLY want to know, don't we, Cheese?'

'YES!' shouted Cheese and half the aircraft turned to look at us. I was going very red, I can tell you.

'The plane doesn't need to flap its wings because it's got very powerful engines that push it through the air.' I nodded and sat back in my seat.

Dad was fluttering his eyelashes at me and he started making baby talk.

'But, Nicky, how does the plane stay up in the air? Because it's vewy heavy like a big lump of lead and big lumps can't fly, can they? So how does a big lumpy thing like a plane do it? Tell us, Nicky, pleeeese!'

I was squirming in my seat. I mean, I learned about aerodynamics and curved wings and air pressure and all that in science lessons at school, but how do you explain it to a three-year-old? Then I had a brainwave.

'Ask Mum,' I said. 'Mums know everything.'

Dad's face fell. 'That's cheating,' he complained.

I just kept my mouth shut, sat back in my seat again and gazed out of the window.

Anyhow, Cheese had completely lost interest by this time because all of a sudden the engines were roaring and we were charging down the runway. The plane's nose went up and *whooosh!* – I love take-off!

Actually, I think take-off and landing are the best bits about flying. That long bit in between is pretty boring. It only gets interesting when the aircrew bring food round or you're watching a film on the seat screen, or something unexpected happens like when the woman two rows ahead of us opened up the overhead baggage locker and the contents of her bag rained down on her because she'd left it in there on its side, wide open. She just crouched there while the bag spewed lipsticks and combs and brushes and scarves and handkerchieves, a pair of comfy shoes, a loose chicken sandwich, an open bag of Maltesers, rolled-up tights, three pairs of knickers, a mini umbrella, another mini umbrella, ANOTHER mini umbrella (how much rain was she expecting?) and a blanket which unfolded and completely enveloped her right down to her knees.

Cheese and Tomato were scrabbling round the floor, hunting for Maltesers that might have rolled their way.

I fell asleep. I think most people did. I didn't wake up until the plane gave a bouncy bump as it landed. NEW YORK! We'd arrived!

We had to queue for a while to get through customs and when Dad showed his passport the customs officer looked at him rather suspiciously.

'Do I know you?' he asked, with a face carved from stone.

Dad shook his head. 'No, not me, but maybe you know my youngest son. His bottom is famous.'

'I beg your pardon?'

'My son has a famous bottom. Loads of people have seen it. Millions and millions.'

'Are you kidding me? Are you some kind of nut?' The customs man was getting angry. It was time for Mum to come to the rescue.

'Sorry, officer. Please ignore my husband, but he's just so proud of our son. We all are.' Mum went on to explain about the WhoTube competition and the officer's face lit up.

'Yeah! I read about that. Of course, there was a photo of you guys. THAT'S where I saw that ugly mug!' He pointed at Dad and then called across to the other officers checking passports.

'Hey! Guess who I've got here? The little guy with the famous bottom! You know, the one going into space? He's here. This is him, right in front of me!'

There was chaos. Everyone crowded round, wanting to catch a glimpse of Cheese. One of the other customs men looked at Cheese's passport and pulled a face.

U.S.
CUSTOMS
NO SMILING

'Hey, this picture ain't nothin' like him. It's his face! He should have his famous bottom in his passport!'

Everyone fell about laughing and we were practically swept through customs control and out to the front of the airport.

'There you go, little fella, and the rest of you

folks. Have a good time now and welcome to
America!'

We were left staring at the taxi rank and the
long, long queue of people waiting for rides. We
had just started walking to the end of the queue
when a man looking like an escaped bear wearing
a peaked cap came running up.

'You de WhoToob family?' he asked in a deep, husky, Italian voice. 'I tort so. You come with me now. Car's round de corner.'

We followed him and there it was. Actually, it looked like about five cars stuck together. It was a stretch limo, a pure white stretch limo.

'I feel like the Queen,' sighed Mum with a smile.

'You are a queen – my queen,' said Dad.

'One, two, three – *YUURRRK!*' went the twins as Mum gave Dad a kiss.

The driver picked up ALL our bags in his massive arms and shoved them in the boot, or

rather the 'trunk', as they call it in the States. The trunk looked big enough to put a whole house in, and the garden too.

Getting into the limo was like going into a cave. There were vast seats and cupboards everywhere filled with drinks and refreshments. Music was playing and there were twinkly lights that kept changing colour and a big TV screen. There was even a chandelier in the middle!

Dad had to have a play with everything and he kept pressing buttons to see what would happen. Suddenly the roof slid back and we could see

the skyscrapers towering over us like dinosaurs.
Then the seat we were on started to slide
forward until it became a bed. It was all
SO COOL!

I was just getting used to everything when we
stopped at our hotel. A doorman with a top hat
stepped forward and opened the car door for us.
'Welcome! I understand you are the WhoTube
family?'

'Yes,' said Dad. 'This is Mrs WhoTube and
these are the WhoTube children, and I'm Ugly
Mug apparently.'

The doorman gave Dad a tolerant smile and
showed us through to the desk where we got
booked in and taken up to our room. Did I say
room? I meant rooms. There were six! There
was a main bedroom, two smaller bedrooms, a
living space with views across the city (because
we were on the twenty-second floor!), a
bathroom and a dressing room, where we put all
our clothes.

We just wandered round and round, going, 'Ooh, look at this!' and 'Wow!' and 'Amazing!' Cheese and Tomato raced from one room to another, jumping on anything that appeared the least bit bouncy, including Dad and myself. There was a great swing chair hanging on a chain from the ceiling in the living area. The beds all looked big enough for about ten people. The windows were floor to ceiling. The TV screen took up an entire wall. As for the bath, that was more like a swimming pool. I was surprised there wasn't a diving board at one end.

Finally, we sat down in the armchairs or lounged on the beds and gradually things got quieter and quieter until we realized that Cheese and Tomato had fallen asleep, cuddled together in the swing chair. Dad was slumped forward with his head between his knees, making little snuffling, snoring noises and muttering to himself. 'Am I ugly? No I'm not. I'm not ugly. No. No. *Snnnnrrrrrr!* NO! *Snnnnrrrrrrr!*'

Mum sighed. 'Peace at last,' she murmured as she closed her eyes. And we all fell asleep. Our first time in New York with all its wonderful sights and sounds at our feet and we were fast asleep! Ahhhh!

6. Beware of Dipplypokuses!

We've been exploring. New York is amazing! We went up the Empire State Building, right to the top! The one-hundred-and-second floor! We had to queue for hours to actually get on the viewing platform. Well, it seemed like hours. Cheese and Tomato were almost crying with boredom.

'It'll be worth it when we get there,' Mum told us, but Dad was getting more and more fed up and he kept making daft suggestions.

'I know what to do. I could say I'm allergic to

people and I have to be on the observation deck all alone.'

'What about us, Dad?' I asked.

'OK, OK. How about I tell the officials I've only got five minutes left to live and I must see the view from the top of the building before I die?'

'Nobody will believe you,' Mum told him. 'Just keep quiet and wait, like everyone else. It'll be worth it when we get there.'

'You've already said that,' grumbled Dad.

'That's because it's true. Look, I've still got a couple of bagels in my bag. Eat one of those. Anything to stop you blathering on.'

So Dad ate a bagel and he stopped blathering on for about twenty seconds. Then he started again.

'It'll be Christmas before we get to the front of this queue.'

'It'll be –' began Mum.

'– worth it when we get there,' chanted

Dad. 'Let me have the other bagel. At least it's something to do.'

'I gave it to Cheese and Tomato to share,' said Mum.

'NOOOOO!' wailed Dad. 'The last bagel's been taken from me!'

The woman standing in front of us turned round, gave my father a startled glance and then smiled at Mum. 'Did you say Cheese and Tomato? The famous Cheese and Tomato twins? The one with the famous bottom that's going into space?'

Mum nodded.

'Oh my,' said the woman. 'I can't believe it. Do you mind if I take some pics, maybe a selfie with me and your twins?'

'That's fine,' said Mum.

'Just a moment,' Dad butted in. 'Let's see, how about if you take photos we are allowed to go to the front of the queue?'

'Don't be ridiculous, Ron.' Mum turned back

to the woman, who was getting her phone out of her bag. 'Please ignore my husband. I think his brain has been badly affected by the great height we're at.'

The woman laughed. 'Oh, I've read all about your husband.'

Dad certainly perked up when he heard that. 'Really? Where did you read it? What did it say?'

'It was in some magazine last week. It was about the WhoTube competition so it was mostly about Cheese, of course, but the article was also asking what kind of a father would call his children Cheese and Tomato.'

Dad raised his eyebrows a fraction. 'Oh? And did they have an answer to that?'

'They did,' said the woman. 'But it wasn't very flattering.'

Dad thought for a few moments. 'The thing is, you see, you Americans have a very different sense of humour to us British. You don't understand ours at all.'

'I am British,' the woman said. 'And the magazine was too.'

'Oh.'

Dad went quiet after that and the woman took some pictures of herself with Cheese and Tomato. Then she took some of herself with the twins and me and Mum. She asked Dad if he'd like to be in the picture too, but Dad waved her phone aside.

'I'm not very photogenic,' he muttered. 'I've got an ugly mug. I'll probably break your mobile.'

'He's sulking,' Mum told the woman. 'Pay no attention.'

At last the queue moved forward and we were able to go out on to the observation deck.

Oh boy! It was amazing. We could see the whole of New York spread out below us.

'Isn't it beautiful?' said Mum. 'You can see everything. I said it would be worth the wait.'

'You did indeed,' agreed Dad. 'About fifty times. Anyhow, I'll tell you something you can't see. King Kong. Where's King Kong? I thought he was supposed to be clinging to the top of the Empire State Building?'

'Very funny, Dad.'

'You can see as far as 'Stralia!' Tomato shouted.

'Are you sure?' asked Mum. 'How do you know?'

'Cos I can see a garoo.'

'Goodness, I didn't know there were kangaroos in New York,' Mum told her.

'Not New York! It's in 'Stralia!'

'Oh right. Well, you've certainly got amazing

eyesight if you can see as far as Australia,' Mum laughed.

'And I can see a . . . a . . . a dipplypokus!' shouted Cheese, not wanting to be outdone.

'A dipplypokus? That's scary.'

'It's eating the cars!'

'Really? I thought diplodocuses only ate vegetables.' Mum gave Cheese a questioning look and he frowned.

'This dipplypokus eats cars,' he said firmly, and to make sure Mum understood how serious this was he added, 'and people.'

'In that case I'm glad we're safe at the top of this very high building where diplodocuses can't reach us.'

'Yes,' nodded Cheese and he went back to staring out over the city.

We stayed up there for ages. There was so much to see. Eventually, Dad suggested we should head off to Central Park and have a picnic, so we did. The park is huge and it's got lots of ponds and lakes. We went to the biggest one called The Lake because you can hire rowing boats there.

Dad and I took it in turns to row. It was hard work, especially when Dad started pretending that all the other boats on the Lake were enemy ships.

'Load the cannon!' He yelled to the twins and they pretended to stuff cannonballs into a cannon.

'Fire! *BOOOOOOOM!*

SPERLASSHH!

Missed! Quick, load up again. Fire! *BOOOOOM!*
KERRBANNGGG! Direct hit! Well done, twins!
Now we'll get that one over there. Load up!'

I think the Battle of Central Park Lake lasted
about half an hour, by which time Dad reckoned
he'd sunk almost everyone else in sight and was
now Ruler of the Waves. Then he decided we
were explorers heading into unknown territory,
sailing up a river infested with alligators,
piranhas, anacondas and giant aquatic spiders.

Dad stood at the bow of our boat, pretending
he was holding a telescope. 'Keep rowing, Nicky.
Don't make those oars splash or you'll disturb the
piranha fish and they'll leap out of the water and
bite your nose.'

'I don't think piranhas can leap, Dad,'
I pointed out.

'Obviously, you have never met the Giant Jumping Piranhas of Central Park Lake. Look! There's one now!'

Dad pointed at a small piece of bread floating on the surface that the ducks had managed to miss. Cheese and Tomato immediately screamed and scrambled to the other side of the boat, making it rock crazily, and before we knew it Dad had lost his balance.

'Whoa – *Nooooo!*'

SPER-LASHHHH!

Dad floundered about, spurting water from his mouth.

'Daddy! Hurry! The Jumping Bananas will bite you!!' Cheese yelled anxiously, waving his arms.

Dad splashed towards us and held on to the side of the boat. Slowly, he hauled himself back and lay in the bottom in a big pool of water. A large piece of waterweed was clinging to his shoulder.

'How do you do it?' asked Mum. 'I am speechless, Ron. Every time we go somewhere you manage to fall into something or bang your head or break something. It's extraordinary.'

'Maybe he should be in the *Big Book of World Records* for having more accidents than anyone else,' I suggested.

Mum laughed. 'He'll certainly get in the *Big Book of Records* for being the soggiest dad in the world.'

'Ha ha,' said Dad. 'Very funny, I don't think.'

We rowed back to shore and ate our picnic on the grass, while Dad lay in a patch of sun and tried to dry off.

After that we wandered around until Dad had more or less stopped squelching and Mum decided it was all right to go back to the hotel. It was our last night. The next day we would be setting off for Florida and the Kennedy Space Center. Whoopee!

7. Hellyboppers

We flew from New
York to Orlando,
Florida. Mum was
wondering if we'd be
collected from the airport
by a super-long limo again.

'I liked that,' she said.

But there was no limo.
Instead, we were met by a
short, slim woman wearing
a smart orangey uniform
with a cluster of badges
on both sleeves and
across her chest. They
made her look quite
important.

'Hi, I'm Commander Anders from NASA and I'm your guide for the time you're with us. Please call me Cassie. I'm going to take you to your hotel to settle in. I'll pick you up tomorrow morning at nine and then the fun starts. You've got a couple of pretty full days ahead of you at Kennedy Space Center. Any questions, just ask.'

Dad put his hand in the air as if he was a schoolboy. 'Yes, I have one. I've always wanted to know what happens if you turn an octopus inside out?'

Commander Anders looked at Dad, her eyes like laser beams, while Mum turned red with embarrassment, I bit my lip and even the twins fell silent.

'If you turn an octopus inside out?' repeated Cassie. Dad nodded.

'It dies.'

'Right,' muttered Dad.

Cassie paused before saying, 'Questions like that – you know, octopuses and so on – well, they're a bit out of my frame of reference, sir. I'm an astronaut, OK? So if you have any more queries of that nature then I suggest you ask your kids.'

Mum burst out laughing and had to clap a hand over her mouth as people turned to look. 'Oh, Ron! She's really got you taped! Bravo, Cassie!'

'There's a joker in every pack, ma'am,' said the commander.

The two women exchanged smiles and Mum told Cassie that she looked super fit and far too young to be a space commander.

'I'm forty-two, ma'am,' Cassie said proudly. 'I train hard. You have to be more than fit to be an astronaut. I swim two miles every day before breakfast. I do push-ups and pull-ups until I wish I didn't have any arms at all. I lift weights, cycle, row – everything.'

'And it shows,' Mum beamed. 'You must be so proud of what you've achieved.'

'I sure am, ma'am.'

I wanted to know what all Cassie's badges were for so she went through some of them. 'This one here is my ranking badge, showing that I'm a commander. That means most of the guys in lower ranks have to take off their hats when I walk past – I'm cool with that! These four badges are for the missions I've been on. I flew one shuttle mission before they stopped those and I've been up to the International Space Station three times. This one here is my Astronaut Wings. Now I've a question for you guys. Which one of you has the famous bottom?' She threw a glance at Dad. 'I take it it's not you, sir?'

Now it was Dad's turn to go red and he bloomed like a rose, coughed and shook his head vigorously.

'Thank the Lord for that!' grinned Cassie and fixed her eyes on the twins. 'It's one of you fellas, isn't it? But which one?'

'ME!' cried Cheese.

Cassie glanced up at Mum. 'What is it about guys and their bottoms? Oh well, lots to do so we'd best get a move on. This way, folks. Fall in line, quick time!'

I liked Cassie. She was a straightforward, no-messing-about kind of person. No wonder Dad had gone unusually quiet in her presence.

Cassie led us out of the airport where we piled into an SUV along with our luggage. She drove off at high speed, not joining the highway, but arcing round the edge of the airport and racing across open ground towards a large hangar. Standing outside was a helicopter.

My heart began beating faster. I was thinking, *No, no. Surely we're not going in a helicopter!*

'Any of you guys been in a chopper before?' Cassie asked, half turning in her seat.

'No!' we chorused.

'Then you're in for a treat. It's a great view.'

'Is it safe?' asked Dad.

I was stunned. My dad was asking if it was safe? My dad! The man who'd brought an alligator into the house! The man who'd actually wrestled the very same alligator in the local pond!

'Well, sir,' said Cassie thoughtfully, 'it's a lot safer than going into outer space. I'm game, if you are.'

Some people came trotting out of the hangar, doffing their hats at Cassie. They took our luggage and loaded it into the chopper. We climbed inside and strapped ourselves in. I could feel my heart beating. I was full of nerves and excitement, as if tiny little people were running round and round my insides, shouting nonsense at each other. I looked at Mum and Dad and I could see they were feeling the same. Mum gave me a half-smile and held up her hands to show me she had crossed her fingers. Dad was tugging at his seat belt as if he wanted to make sure it would work in an emergency. The twins were staring out of the windows and calling to each other.

'I can see another hellybopper!' Cheese was pointing across the field.

''Nother hellybopper,' echoed Tomato.

Cassie climbed into the pilot's seat.

'You can fly copters AND spacecraft?' asked Mum. 'They never taught *me* that at school.'

Cassie laughed. 'Nor me! But, you know, joining the air force and then coming to work with the space agency is like being given one enormous play area to run about in. I used to dream about this as a child and now I'm doing it, living my dream. I'm very lucky. OK, guys, time for lift-off.'

Cassie began flicking switches and pressing buttons. I glanced over her shoulder. I had never seen so many knobs and dials and buttons and levers. Little lights showed up on some of the panels and dials flickered into life. The rotors began to turn, so slowly at first, and then the swoosh turned to a clatter and the clatter became a roar. With a jerk and a jump, we lifted into the air.

It was so different from being in a big plane. First of all, you could feel every tiny move and little bump, every breath of wind as we rose higher and higher. The helicopter seemed to vibrate from one end to the other and we all vibrated with it. The view was amazing! We could see right out to the Atlantic Ocean.

The nose of the chopper dipped a fraction and we went charging forward, swooping over Cape Canaveral and then up to the Kennedy

Space Center itself. Cassie circled round so
we had a bird's-eye view of everything. It was
stupendous! She gave us a non-stop description
of what we were looking at before heading back
inland to skim over Orlando so that we could
look down on the skyscrapers, lakes and all the
theme parks that seemed to stretch for miles.

'And now for your hotel,' Cassie announced as
we dipped down to the city, where the evening
lights were just beginning to flicker into life.

Guess where we landed? Only on the hotel
roof! Amazing! We waited until the rotor blades

had stopped turning and then jumped out. We crossed over to a lift and zipped down to the hotel reception before we went whizzing back up to the fifteenth floor and another miniature indoor house, with three bedrooms and a kitchen and living area, bathroom and so on. All the bedrooms were bigger than *any* of our rooms at home! The bathroom had two showers and two baths in it. Maybe the hotel wanted to make sure their guests were VERY clean. Not only that, but there was an outside balcony with – guess what? A barbecue! We had our own outdoor barbecue on the fifteenth floor!

We settled in and raided the fridge for snacks and drinks while Cheese and Tomato went racing round from one room to another.

Mum lounged back on the huge sofa and looked across at Dad, who was staring out of the window at the rest of Orlando.

'You've been very quiet for a while,' said Mum. 'Ever since Cassie got the measure of you, you've hardly said a word.'

'Cassie? What are you talking about?' Dad blustered.

'You know perfectly well. All that stuff she said about being a joker in the pack and suggesting you were behaving like a child.'

'She didn't say that.'

'You're right, Ron, she didn't say it. But you and I know that's what she meant.'

Dad sighed and his shoulders seemed to slump. 'The thing is, you can't joke with someone who doesn't have a sense of humour,' he complained.

Mum shook her head. 'Cassie does have a sense of humour. It's just different from yours. You crack jokes that make our children laugh. You can't expect grown-ups to find the same things funny. And she's right – there is a bit of the child in you.'

Mum smiled, got up, went across to Dad and put her arms round him. 'Don't fret,' she told him. 'Cassie flies spacecraft, for heaven's sake! That's serious stuff. You can't expect her to laugh at your silly jokes. But don't worry – I shall. You make me laugh, Ron, and the children and I love that part of you, so stop worrying. Just be yourself and give me a kiss.'

Cheese and Tomato looked at me in alarm. Tomato shouted out, 'One, two, three –'

And I joined in too.

'URRRRRGH!!'

8. Which Way Do Rockets Go?

Dad's his old self today. I think it was the size of the hotel breakfast. As soon as he saw it, his face exploded into the most enormous grin. He got himself a plate with two fried eggs, three slices of bacon, three hash browns, four sausages, a pile of mushrooms, a heap of tomatoes, a mountain of beans, four slices of toast and a large green gherkin.

Mum looked at his plate and shuddered. 'A gherkin? For breakfast?'

'I like gherkins,' said Dad.

Mum shuddered again and then tried to look angelic. 'I've got some fresh fruit and yoghurt. When I've eaten my fresh fruit and yoghurt I shall feel fresh and —'

'Yoghurty,' Dad jumped in. 'You'll feel yoghurty, which is a horribly sloppy and disgustingly sludgy sensation.'

'Not at all. I shall be as fresh and light as a feather on a baby duck, whereas you will be ten kilograms heavier and look like the back end of a large buffalo, because that's what you've just eaten.'

'Not at all,' Dad echoed. 'I shall be fuelled up for the day with all that protein, whereas you will stutter and putter along for about five minutes before fainting from weakness and complaining that you need something proper to eat, like a plate of steak and chips.'

Mum scowled, took another spoonful of

yoghurt and muttered something dark about gherkins while Dad whistled a jaunty tune and cut up his sausages.

So things were back to normal!

As soon as breakfast was over, we were collected by Cassie.

'Hey, hi! How are you guys this morning? Lots to do at the Center today. I hope you're fighting fit?'

'I'm tip-top,' said Dad.

Cassie grinned. 'You British have such a funny way of saying things.' She dipped her head slightly and repeated, 'Tip-top! That's so cute.'

'Yes,' said Dad. 'I'm fine, but I'm afraid my wife might collapse at any moment.'

Alarm flooded Cassie's face. 'But she looks OK.'

'I know,' said Dad. 'She does now, but she only had some fruit and yoghurt for breakfast so I don't expect her to last long.'

Cassie shook her head. 'There really is no stopping you, is there?'

Dad grinned. 'Nope!'

'Come on,' sighed Cassie. 'Let's head for the stars.'

There was no helicopter this time, just a big SUV. We piled in and drove out to the Space Center.

IT IS HUMONGOUSLY HUGE!

(In other words – big!!)

The buildings were big. The rockets were big.

The crowds were big. Even the queues at the main attractions were big, but we were VIPs. (That means Very Important Persons!) Once we were parked up, Cassie took us straight to the front of every queue. It was bliss! Plus, all the people in the queue would stare at us, wondering who we were, like we were film stars or something, and it was all because of Cheese's bottom!

Inside we just stood there, our eyes on stalks.
Right in front of us, hanging in mid-air as if it
was flying, was a full-sized space shuttle. It wasn't
a model. It was a REAL SPACE SHUTTLE,
one that had actually flown all the way up there
in space. Cool!

'OK,' said Cassie. 'Here we are at the Space
Training Experience. First up is rocket building.
You're going to learn how to build an air-
powered rocket and we'll see who makes the most
powerful one.'

Dad's eyes started to glow. He loves that kind
of competition – and so do I! We looked at each
other. Our eyes locked. Our brows knitted. Our
chins jutted. We gritted our teeth. It was Dad
versus me!

We got down to it. Building the rocket was
pretty straightforward. We had a long, thin piece
of plastic tubing sealed at the top end. We stuck
fins round the bottom so what we had made was
basically like a fat, hollow arrow. A helper came

round, giving us advice and handing over equipment. We were given a fat cork with a hole through the middle. That plugged into the bottom of the missile. A long piece of rubber tubing went through the hole into the body of the rocket. The other end was attached to a large air pump.

All around us other families were building their rockets. Some people had started launching and every so often there'd be a *pop* and a *whoosh* as a rocket took off and arced across the room. I was sure I could get higher than any of them. So was Dad!

He looked
at me. I looked
at Dad. We were
ready.

'You go first,'
he said.

I started pumping. It
was harder than I thought.
I was beginning to wonder if
my rocket would ever take off
and then suddenly –

BOPP!

SHWOOOOOOOOMM!

My rocket was brilliant! It went really
high, almost reaching the roof before it
came clattering back down.

It was Dad's turn. He rolled up his sleeves. He jogged on the spot. He swung his arms round and round. He got down on the floor and did ten press-ups. He went across to his rocket, bowed before it and declared in a loud voice: 'I name this rocket THE WINNER!'

Dad started pumping. He pumped and he pumped. He pumped until his face was scarlet and his eyes were bulging and his beard was on fire. (Well, not the beard bit – but he did go very red!)

BOPP!

SHWOOOOooooofff!!

Dad's rocket went shooting off sideways,
crazily zigzagging through the air just above

the heads of some of the other rocket builders,
making them duck in fear of their heads being

taken off. It suddenly veered sideways and up,
clanged against the space shuttle, making it

tremble, and all the audience went 'OOOH!'
and 'AHHH!' until eventually it buried itself

in an astronaut's suit that was hanging on a display stand. Very slowly, the stand began to topple backwards, gaining momentum, and then *KERRUMPPPP!* the whole thing fell to the ground.

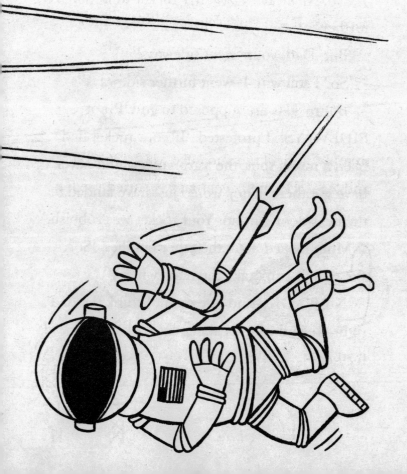

Now everyone was staring at the rocket. Then they turned to gawp just as hard at Dad. He was beaming from ear to ear and punching the air with both fists.

'I won! I won!' he crowed.

'No, Dad, *I won*. My rocket went higher than yours.'

'No, Nicky, no. *I won*. My rocket went much further.'

'But, Dad, yours went sideways!'

'So? I still win. It went further sideways!'

'But rockets are supposed to go UP, not SIDEWAYS!' I protested. 'If your rocket had been a moon shot, the astronauts would never have got there. They would just have landed in the next-door garden. Your rocket was rubbish.'

Mum looked at all the other families. 'Sorry,' she said. 'I can't take them anywhere.'

'No, it's OK,' said one man. 'I think the dad's right. Technically speaking, his rocket did travel further.'

'That's so not fair,' a little girl cried. 'The boy's rocket went up to the roof. That's a long way. The boy won. The boy won!' She was almost in tears.

Then they all weighed in. Soon everyone was shouting and there were even a few people pushing and shoving each other as they argued.

'The boy's the winner!'

'Are you crazy? The old man won, hands down!'

Suddenly there was a loud crackle as a loudspeaker system came on.

'Would you all just settle down?! This is a space centre, not a zoo! You're lucky you won't all be arrested for damaging a multimillion-dollar space shuttle, not to mention a display of spacesuits.'

For three seconds the crowd was silent. Then they turned on Dad.

'BUT HE DID IT!' everyone shouted. 'It wasn't us. It was him!' A hundred fingers pointed at Dad, who put his hands in his pockets and started whistling innocently.

'IT DOESN'T MATTER WHO DID IT!' roared the speakers and I was pretty sure I recognized Commander Cassie's voice. 'Please go back to your own rocket at once. The Famous Bottom Family, please go straight through to the Education Center next door.'

The loudspeakers crackled off and people began asking each other who had a famous bottom. It wasn't long before they were getting upset again.

'How dare you ask me about my bottom!'

'I wasn't! I just wanna know who's got a famous one.'

'Well, it's certainly not mine, so stop looking! What I do with my bottom is none of your business.'

Meanwhile, we crept quietly away to the Education Center where Commander Cassie was waiting for us. She did not look happy.

'I've never seen anything like it,' she said, shaking her head.

'All I did was follow the instructions and make

a rocket,' Dad protested. 'I don't know why it went sideways and I didn't ask anyone to start arguing on my behalf. And, I might add,' he went on rather wickedly, '*I* wasn't the one who mentioned famous bottoms.'

All of which was quite true. Dad was right. He *hadn't* meant to start anything. It had just happened, out of nowhere, like a magician's trick. The sort of magician you definitely wouldn't invite to a children's party.

'OK,' sighed Cassie, calming down a little. 'We'll take a lunch break and then this afternoon we'll be on the Gravity Swing. Do try and keep things relaxed and easy, hey?'

'We can try,' agreed Mum. But she didn't sound very hopeful.

9. Mum Ties Herself Up

The Gravity Swing was sensational. It was meant
to imitate the gravity you find on the moon.
Have you ever seen those films of astronauts
walking on the moon? If you have you'll know
that they don't take footsteps at all. They take
foot-bounces!

'Gravity on the moon isn't the same as that
on Earth. Our gravity is about six times more
powerful than gravity on the moon. So here's a
little test for you guys. If you build a rocket –'
Cassie broke off at that point and fixed Dad with
her laser eyes – 'if you build a rocket and it flies
one hundred metres on Earth, how far will it fly
on the moon?'

'Six hundred metres,' I answered, very proud
of myself.

'Right, at least in theory,' said Cassie. 'In fact, it would travel even further than that because there is very little atmosphere on the moon to slow it down. But six hundred metres is near enough. What the Gravity Swing does is recreate what you would experience on the moon. It does this using elastic webbing and a system of weights and pulleys in the roof. Just get yourselves strapped into the harness and off you go. You will be walking on the moon.'

It was brilliant! I went first. A man helped me to strap the belt round my waist and told me to hold on to the straps that went up to the roof, and I was off. It felt really weird at first and very funny, because it was like you were a balloon bouncing around. There was a moon-like surface to cross and every time you took the smallest step you would take off. If you tried to take an ordinary step you almost ended up on the other side of the room! It took very little effort to move and, once you were used to it, it felt almost calm

and peaceful.
What a lovely way
to go for a walk.
Jumping was even
more brilliant. It
was like being able
to leap over trees!

'I want a go!'
Cheese shouted.

'I want a go!'
Tomato echoed.

A security man
stepped forward.
'Sorry. Children
under ten years
old are not
allowed on this
equipment.'

Cheese stared
up at the guard.
His lower lip

began to quiver. 'I want a go,' he repeated
very quietly.

Tomato clutched at the man's leg. 'Want a go,'
she whispered and they both stared up at him
with wet, doggy eyes.

But the guard didn't like dogs and he was
unmoved. Cheese could see there was no chance.
He held Tomato's hand and pulled her away.
He murmured something in her left ear. Tomato
glanced at the guard and grinned. A determined
look quickly replaced the grin and suddenly the
twins were off, racing at high speed towards the
Gravity Swing.

'Stop!' yelled the guard, hotfooting it after
them in his big boots. The twins didn't get far.
The guard overtook them and swept them up,
one tucked under each arm. He turned to Mum
and Dad.

'Your children,' he scowled.

'Well, you seem to have them nicely under
control,' Dad remarked. 'I have to say it's

remarkable you don't have a separate Gravity
Swing for small children. It's obvious that every
child will want to have a go, not just those over
ten. Everybody likes a good bounce.'

The guard gritted his teeth and growled. 'I
never bounce,' he declared. 'I'm an adult.'

'I know,' sighed Dad. 'And that's where the problem lies. Come on,' he added, turning to Mum. 'Your turn next, while this kind man looks after the twins.'

Dad helped Mum into the harness while the twins watched and whimpered and wriggled in the guard's grasp.

'This is wonderful!' Mum cried, bouncing up and down. 'It reminds me of when I used to go trampolining as a child. I won a medal, you know, when I was ten. It was for the best mid-air somersaults. I bet I can still do them too.'

Mum took a few small steps and then jumped up into the air, tried to do a forward somersault and ended up with both arms and one leg caught up in the webbing. She began to bounce up and down pointlessly, struggling all the while to get herself out of the knot she was in.

'I just need to do a backward somersault to untie myself,' she panted. 'If I can just get one foot on the ground to give myself a bit of a boost –'

Mum did get
one foot on the
ground. She
pushed as hard as
she could, went
zooming up into
the air, tried to
do a backward
somersault
and ended up
completely,
hopelessly knotted,
with all her arms
and legs now
bound up with
elastic and her
head poking out
from somewhere
below, in a
lopsided kind
of way.

'Help,' she managed to squeak.

I ran across to Cassie, who was busy talking to a family that had just arrived.

'Cassie! My mum – she's in a spot of bother. She's got a bit tied up.'

Cassie looked over at the Gravity Swing. A frown crinkled her brow before sliding down her nose and settling on her mouth. 'Nicky,' she said, 'you poor boy. How do you cope?'

'Sorry?' I had no idea what she meant.

'How do you manage with parents like yours? First it was your father and now it's your mother.'

I shrugged and then remembered something I'd read somewhere.

'You can choose your friends, but you can't choose your parents, can you? Besides, I wouldn't swap them for anything. My mum and dad are the best in the world.'

Cassie gave a funny kind of grunt. 'Sure. Of course they are, kid. OK, let's go rescue your mom.'

106

So Cassie went off to help Mum while I rescued the security guard from the twins.

'You're a bad man!' shouted Tomato as I took her hand. The guard scowled in silence.

It took ten minutes to untangle Mum. Once she had both feet back on the ground she looked at Cassie and pulled an embarrassed face. 'Sorry,' she murmured.

Cassie shook her head and laughed. 'It's no wonder you Brits never managed to conquer space.'

Dad tapped Cassie on the shoulder. 'Excuse me? Correction: at least two Britons have been into space and the United Kingdom Space Agency is helping develop the Skylon spaceplane, a plane actually invented by a British company. We might be a small country, but we have DREAMS.' Dad thumped his chest with his fist.

'Bravo!' Mum cried, clapping her hands.

'I didn't know that, Dad. Is it true?'

'Yes, Nicky. It's quite true.'

I thought, *Wow! We're developing a spaceplane! I wonder where it is.*

Cassie took a step back and looked at us with pride. She was actually proud of us for once!

'Hey, that's so cool. I didn't know that. Thank you for telling me.' She put a hand on Dad's shoulder. 'And you know, sir, dreams are very important. It's dreams that made me become an astronaut.'

Dad nodded. 'Yep. And it's dreams that made me a . . . a dreamer!'

Cassie laughed. 'OK, now that we have your wife out of the Gravity Swing I guess it's your turn. Try not to knock anything over, sir.'

'I'll do my best,' said Dad.

'That's what we're afraid of,' warned Mum.

As Dad went across to the Gravity Swing, one of the guards stopped him.

'Excuse me, sir,' he began. 'Are you over eighteen?'

'That depends,' answered Dad.

'Sorry?'

'It depends what the eighteen applies to. Am I over eighteen years of age or over eighteen metres tall?'

'Well, sir, I can see you're not over eighteen metres tall.'

'But you can't see that I'm over eighteen years of age? That's strange, but I have to say I'm quite pleased as I'm actually forty-two.'

'OK, sir, you can carry on.'

Dad glanced back at us, pointed at his brain, pulled a face and nodded towards the guard while rolling his eyes.

'Actually, sir, I'm not mad. Just doing my job,' the guard responded.

Dad let himself be strapped in. It was like watching a child in a playground. Actually, it had been much the same for Mum. She'd been like a child too, but at least Dad managed to have fun without tying himself and the harness into knots.

We were pretty tired by the time we'd done all

that. Cassie showed us the rockets they used to fly people to the moon and the spacesuits they wore. It was interesting, but Cheese and Tomato had already fallen asleep so we carefully put them into the SUV and Cassie drove us back to the hotel.

'You all get some sleep now,' she suggested. 'Big day tomorrow. You've got a TV interview in the morning and in the afternoon is the rocket launch. You'll be on the grandstand with all the bigwigs. The president will be there.'

'The President of the United States?' gasped Mum.

'You bet,' grinned Cassie. 'Sleep well!'

Before we went to bed we wrote some postcards home.

Dad sent a postcard to Mr Tugg. Mum sent one to Mrs Tugg. I wrote to Granny and Lancelot, and the twins wrote to nobody in particular.

Dear Mr Tugg,

We're having a lovely time at the Kennedy Space Center, Florida.

We asked the astronauts if they'd ever captured a Martian. To our surprise they said no! We told them that we live right next door to one. They're coming to get you. Watch out! You have been warned.

Best wishes from Ron

Dear Mrs Tugg,

I hope you're both enjoying a bit of peace and quiet while we're away. I also hope that the animals are behaving themselves. We've been for a spin in a helicopter and today we went to the Space Center and practised being astronauts. Tomorrow is the BIG DAY. We're going to meet the president himself and Cheese's bottom will be launched into space!

Love from Brenda and family

Dear Granny and Lancelot,
   It's amazing here! You should see
our hotel! We're on the fifteenth
floor. We've got a BBQ on our
balcony! We've been whizzing about in a
helicopter and we had a stretch limo and
Mum got tied up with elastic and had to
be rescued and Dad almost knocked
a space shuttle over. You would love it
here. It's A-MAZING!
   Love, Nicky
PS Hope Elvis the sheep is behaving
himself.

Dear animals,
HeLlo!
CHeESE
TOmaTo
X X

10. The Very Famous Bottom Family

It was weird being interviewed. Commander Cassie collected us from the hotel after breakfast. She had brought with her some T-shirts from the Space Center and notebooks and pens and stuff.

'You should have been given these mementoes yesterday at the Center, but there was so much going on they forgot.'

I noticed Cassie giving Mum a wink.

'You mean they were too busy stopping the other visitors from tearing each other apart over the rocket fiasco,' chuckled Mum, and Cassie nodded.

'But here they are. One T-shirt for each of you. Even Mom and Dad get one.'

'Cool!' I said, pulling mine on at once.

Dad held his up. 'Tip-top. Tickety-boo. Top-hole, what!'

'You British!' cried Cassie, wide-eyed.

'We don't really talk like my husband,' Mum explained. 'He's just being silly. Again.'

'And it's only half past nine,' added Cassie with a shake of her head. They both burst out laughing. It took Cassie a few moments to recover and then she said, 'We'd best get going. Can't keep the president waiting.'

I gulped. We really were going to meet the President of the United States. What would I say? How do you talk to a President? What do you call a President? My heart was already in my mouth and we were only in the car on the way to the TV station.

I thought we'd go straight to some studio for the interview, but first we had to go to make-up where we sat in chairs while people got all fussy about our hair and stuff. Then someone put powder on my face and brushed it all over my skin because they thought I looked too pale! They tried to do the same with Dad as well, but he pushed them away.

'Geroff! I don't need any of that ladies' stuff!'

'It's just to give you a bit of colour, sir,' the make-up girl told him.

'I don't need any colour, thank you. Just because all you lot have suntans doesn't mean I need an instant one.'

'Don't be so grumpy,' Mum told him, but the make-up staff had already given up on Dad and left him alone.

Once we had been made presentable we went to the waiting area next door. We sat and twiddled our thumbs for ten minutes. There was a big TV screen in the room broadcasting what was happening in the studio at that very moment, so we could see and hear who was being interviewed by the host, Mike Plank. I had butterflies in my stomach, my chest, my brain and my socks. A girl came backstage and beckoned to us. She held a finger to her lips and the next thing we heard was the introduction.

'And now, all the way from Britain, we have – from the top of the WhoTube viewing table – the Very Famous Bottom Family!'

There was applause and the girl pushed us

onstage. The glare of the
lights hit us. It was dazzling
and all I could hear was
Mike Plank.

'Here they are – the
Famous Bottom Family!
We have Mom and Dad
there, and Nicholas,
he's twelve, and finally
the twins, Cheese and
Tomato, just three years old, folks.'

Mike said 'tomato' as if it rhymed with
'potato'.

'It's Cheese, of course, who has the famous
bottom. That's right, guys, you sit yourselves
down there. OK, so before we start there's one
burning question in many people's minds, not
just here in the studio this morning, but right
across America. No doubt many viewers sitting
at home are wondering just why you decided to
call your twins here Cheese and Tomato.'

'Tomah-to,' corrected Dad.

'That's right,' said the host, 'tomato.'

'No,' said Dad, shaking his head. 'You say tomato but I say tomahto.'

'Uh-uh,' argued Mike. 'You say tomahto but I say tomato.'

'All right!' shouted Dad and he started singing!
'You say tomato and I'll say tomahto, I'll say potato and you'll say potahto, tomato, tomahto, potato, potahto . . .'

The audience were clapping and laughing at the same time. Some of them seemed to be in hysterics.

'Ain't these guys just great!' shouted Mike. 'Now then, you still haven't told us how the twins got those crazy names.'

Mum and Dad told the story of the pizza van between them and once again the audience began to snort. Then Mike turned to me and asked what it was like having loopy parents.

'They're not loopy,' I said. 'They're fun. There's always something going on in our house.

Dad brought home a sheep last week.'

'A sheep? Now why would your father do that?'

'That's a good question,' I said, hastily trying to think of an answer. 'It's just something my dad does. He brought home an alligator once. Now we only have a sheep and a goat, five chickens, two rabbits and a tortoise. The sheep's called Elvis.'

'Elvis? Good name. OK, so you live on a farm?' Mike suggested.

'No. We live in a town. The animals are in our back garden.'

'Does everyone in Britain have their backyards stuffed with farm animals called Elvis?' Mike glanced at the audience and raised his eyebrows suggestively.

'No, no. It's just that Dad is different from other people. He's full of ideas. He's an ideas man. At the moment he's aiming to get himself into the *Big Book of World Records*.'

'Really?' said Mike. 'How's he gonna do that?'

'Oh, he's been making the longest piece of spaghetti in the world.'

Some people in the audience began to snigger. Dad had one hand to his forehead. I think he could see where this conversation was going. Mike was grinning at me.

'And how's that been going then? I mean, it must be difficult to make a really long piece of spaghetti. How's Pop here doing so far?'

'Well, his first attempt wasn't so successful,' I admitted.

'Yeah, we heard something about that from Alisha, the lady from WhoTube who came to your house. I believe she got a bit of a shock? Tell us what happened.'

Dad's face was now completely buried in his hands and he'd stuck his fingers in his ears. I took a deep breath.

'Dad was trying to stick spaghetti strands together end to end, using superglue, and Elvis and the goat came into the house. Dad tried to shoo them away and he stood on the superglue without realizing. When he went back to working with the spaghetti the whole packet got stuck to his hands. He looked like some weird monster with bits of pasta poking out all over the place and in every direction. That's when the doorbell rang. Dad went to the door like that and almost gave Alisha a heart attack.'

I hadn't realized that I'd been so taken up with telling the story that I'd got up from my seat and was acting it all out. By the time I sat down again the audience were just about wetting themselves with laughter and Dad had been cringing with embarrassment more and more. Now he was curled up on the floor in a little ball with his jacket pulled over his head, hoping that nobody could see him.

Mike Plank was wiping tears of laughter from his eyes.

'You guys are just hysterical,' he said. 'Is the whole family like this? We haven't even spoken to Cheese yet, the guy with the famous bottom.' He turned to my little brother.

'Now then, you were in an advert for diapers, is that right?'

'No,' said Cheese, looking puzzled.

'Diapers?' Mum repeated quickly. 'Isn't that what you call nappies in America?'

'That's right, ma'am,' said Mike.

'In that case, yes, Cheese was in a nappy advert,' Mum agreed.

'OK, I'll call them nappies. So, Cheese, you wanted to take a break, eh? I know it's hard work doing these adverts. So you went crawling off without your nappy, with your little bare butt on show, and somehow you managed to get on the desk top of the news broadcast in the studio next door?'

'Yes!' shouted Cheese. 'And everyone saw my botty. POO!'

Squeals of laughter erupted, which only encouraged Cheese to say it again. 'POO!' he shouted, even louder. And then he machine-gunned, '*POO-POO-POO-POO!*'

Mike leaned back in his chair. 'There we have it, ladies and gentlemen, a true professional, someone who knows how to work his audience – and he's only three years old!'

The crowd whooped and hollered. By this time Dad had quietly gone back to sitting on the sofa.

Mike now turned his chair towards Tomato. 'OK, young lady, you've been a very quiet, good little girl. But I want to know what it's like to be a member of this family. Your twin brother seems to be well on the way to being a superstar, but you're sitting here all quiet and innocent. Don't you get miffed by all the attention he gets?'

Tomato looked back at Mike with a very serious expression and slowly shook her head.

Mike seemed a bit fazed by Tomato not actually saying anything, so he went on. 'Tell me, what do *you* do? Cheese has his famous bottom. Is there anything special you can do?'

Tomato still didn't speak. She just nodded rather solemnly. Then she did something that none of us had ever seen before. She tucked her knees up under her T-shirt and pulled it right down so her feet vanished from view. She pulled her arms back inside the sleeves until they had completely disappeared. Finally, she managed to withdraw her head into the neck of her T-shirt until you couldn't see her at all. Then she spoke for the first time, from beneath the shirt.

'I'm a tortoise.'

Out came a little bit of her head. Out came her hands and feet. The crowd went wild again. They clapped and shouted and stamped.

Tomato popped out her whole head and grinned at everyone.

'The very talented Famous Bottom Family!' cried Mike. 'And we wish you good fortune with the space launch this afternoon and you're all going to meet the president, I believe. You show the president your tortoise impression, young lady. I'm sure he'll be pretty amazed.' Mike turned to the audience. 'A big hand for the Famous Bottom Family all the way from Britain!'

11. The President of the United States (and his Wife)

'I have never been so embarrassed in my life,' Dad told us after the interview.

Cassie patted his back. 'It was great TV,' she said. 'Everyone loved it and they loved all of you. You're a hit!'

'I feel as if I've *been* hit,' Dad moaned.

'There, there. You'll recover,' Mum chuckled. 'I must say it seems odd that we keep getting called the Famous Bottom Family. I think when we get back to Britain we shall have to change our names to Mr and Mrs Famous Bottom.'

'You speak for yourself,' said Dad.

Mum chuckled. 'Come on, let's get some lunch. That will cheer you up.'

She was right. By the time we'd eaten a good

meal Dad was back to his old self.

'I can't believe I sang *"You say tomato and I'll say tomahto"* on American TV,' he grinned.

'Neither can we,' said Mum. 'You're a clown, through and through.'

'And Tomato was such a brilliant tortoise,' Dad added fondly.

Tomato immediately did her tortoise impression all over again, except when she popped her head out this time she shouted, 'Daddy stinky-poo!' which got half the restaurant staring at us. It seemed we couldn't go anywhere without attracting unwanted attention – mostly because of the twins.

So the time passed and we began to talk less and less to each other until there was just silence and we were all thinking the same thing. We were about to meet the President of the United States.

Eventually, Mum whispered, 'I have no idea what to say. Do you think his wife will be there too?'

'Don't know,' muttered Dad.

'I'm going to be a tortoise,' Tomato told us.

'I'm going to be, to be a . . . a dipplypokus!' Cheese suddenly decided.

'That should be interesting,' Mum remarked and we all fell silent again.

We were quite glad when Cassie came to get us. At least we were now doing something. We drove, mostly in silence, out to the Space Center. I think we were all staring out of the window, wondering what it would be like.

Well, I can tell you what it was like. I had never seen so many big black cars and big men in dark suits. They were all milling around the podium where the meeting and the launch were going to take place. As soon as we arrived, we were checked all over by security.

'Whatever you do, don't make any jokes about guns or bombs or anything like that,' warned Cassie. 'If you do you'll find yourself whisked away from here and stuck in jail faster than you can say zip-a-dee-doo-dah.'

'Zip –' Dad managed before Mum clamped a firm hand over his mouth.

'Not another sound!' she hissed.

Dad looked at us and pulled such a funny face that we couldn't help giggling.

'And don't you dare laugh at your dad,' Mum snapped. 'It only encourages him.'

We were escorted across to the podium. We climbed up the steps to the top. I was so glad Commander Cassie was still with us. Cheese and

Tomato were holding Mum's hands. Don't tell anyone, but almost without realizing it I found myself holding Cassie's. I was embarrassed, but I didn't want to let go, so I didn't. In the distance we could see the rocket that was going to carry all the different information about Earth and all the messages from around the world into deepest space, maybe to be picked up by aliens in some distant galaxy. And that included the video of Cheese's bottom.

A big, long, black car swept up to the podium. The guard of honour went into full salute mode and snapped into statue formation. Two men ran to the rear doors either side of the limousine.

The president stepped out from one side and his wife from the other.

They were both smiling. Mrs President looked rather elegant.

'I wonder who does her hair,' whispered Mum.

Dad grunted back, 'Ask her.'

The presidential couple came to the podium steps and made their way up. I took a deep breath. This was it. There was no escape. I took another deep breath. I heard Cassie start speaking.

'Good afternoon, Mr President, Mrs President. I'm Commander Cassie Anders and it's my pleasure and privilege to introduce you to the Famous Bottom Family from Britain.'

And suddenly there we were, Mr and Mrs Famous Bottom and their children, shaking hands with the President of the United States, and Mum said: 'I like your hair.'

The president beamed back at her. 'Why, thank you, ma'am. I'm sure that the good people of America will be happy to know that their president has a good barber!'

Mum turned scarlet. 'Oh!' she moaned. 'I meant to say that to your wife!'

'That's OK, ma'am,' the president went on.
'My wife has a fine hairdo too!'

The president and his wife looked at each other
and suddenly everyone was laughing and Tomato
pushed herself forward, pulled at Mrs President's
leg and piped up, 'I can be a tortoise!'

'Really?' said Mrs President. 'I would love to
see that!' So Tomato showed everyone.

'You have lovely children,' Mrs President said

after Tomato had poked her head back out from
her T-shirt.

'I know,' said Mum, smiling at us. 'It's my
husband I worry about.'

'Oh, me too,' agreed the president's wife. 'I
never know what he's going to do next!'

'Mine brought home a sheep last week.'

'A sheep? You were lucky. I was given an army
tank! It was a gift from some country or other. He

comes home with this tank and he says: "Honey, can you put this somewhere for me?" And I say: "Sure, I'll put it in the tank cupboard with all the others!"' They burst out laughing again.

Meanwhile, my dad was having a very interesting conversation with the president, who looked rather thoughtful.

'Yep, I can see your problem,' nodded Mr President. 'Do you think it would be easier if you cooked the spaghetti first and then tried joining it together while it's all floppy?'

'I'll try that,' said Dad. 'That's good advice. Now is there anything I can help *you* with?'

But at that moment someone from the Space Agency came up and interrupted, so Dad's chance to solve some of the world's problems vanished.

'Excuse me, Mr President, sir, it's almost time to launch. We only have a window of a few seconds to get the right trajectory. Could you all please move over to the launch desk? You'll hear

the countdown from twenty and this is the
button here.'

'The red one?'

'That's correct, sir.'

The president got us into a huddle and
made sure that we all had a hand on top of his.
There was the president's hand hovering over
the button. On top of that was Mrs President's
hand, then Mum's, Dad's, mine, then Cheese's
and Tomato's. The countdown began over the
loudspeaker. When we got to ten the crowd
joined in.

'Five, four, three, two, one, BLAST-OFF!'

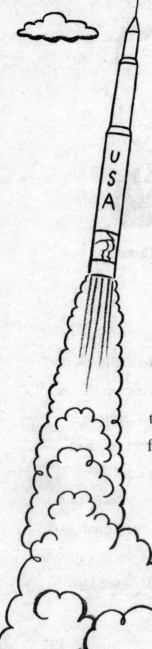

'We have ignition,' went
the loudspeaker as a mighty
roar and vast plumes of smoke
and steam billowed out from
beneath the rocket and then it
was moving. 'We have lift-off!'

It was in the air and racing
up into the sky, faster and faster,
leaving a huge, white, glorious
trail. Cheese's bottom was
heading for outer space and the
longest journey that it would
ever make.

We watched in silence until
the rocket became a speck and
finally disappeared forever.

Cheese tugged at Mum's hand.
'Can I be a dipplypokus now?'

12. A Shocking Arrival

The next day Cassie said goodbye to us in the airport hall. We were all a bit quiet. We didn't really want to leave, especially as we now knew we had a long, boring flight back home.

'I shall miss you all,' Cassie said, rather surprised at herself.

'More likely you'll be glad to see the back of us,' Mum hinted, but the commander shook her head.

'It's sure been a blast having you around. I mean, OK, so there have been some ups and downs –'

'Especially on the Gravity Swing,' Dad put in.

'Especially that,' agreed Cassie. 'And then there was the brawl over the rockets, but you certainly made a difference to my routine. I would have been doing the usual day-to-day stuff, but you guys have been sheer entertainment from start to finish. Thank you.'

A loud announcement boomed round the hall.

'Sounds like your plane has been called,' said Cassie. 'Time to say goodbye.' She gave Mum a big hug and then me and the twins, even Dad.

Dad grinned at her. 'Tip-top!' he said. 'Toodle-pip!'

'You big kook!' laughed Cassie and she reached up and kissed his cheek.

'*URRRGH!*' chorused the twins, while Dad turned crimson with delight.

He took hold of the luggage trolley and we set off for our plane.

I won't bore you with the journey because it bored me to sleep. All I will say is that when we landed back in Britain there was a bit of a shock waiting for us.

Everything was fine until we got to passport

control. Mum was waved through. The twins were waved through. I was waved through. Dad was stopped. What now?

'Please step aside, sir,' ordered the customs officer.

'Sorry? Why? What's up?' Dad was confused.

'Just step over here, sir. Thank you. Can you confirm that you are the person shown on this passport and that this *is* your passport?'

'Of course I can.' Dad gave a nervous laugh. 'What's going on?'

At first the customs officer didn't answer. Instead, he called over two policemen standing nearby. By this time everyone queueing up to go through passport control was staring at us. The policemen stood either side of Dad. The customs officer waved Dad's passport at him.

'There's a warrant out for your arrest, sir,' said the officer.

'WHAT?!' Dad's shout went off like a hand grenade. 'You've got to be joking! I haven't done anything. What on earth are you arresting me for?'

'Sheep rustling, sir.'

'SHEEP RUSTLING?'

The penny dropped. I think we all understood at the same time just what had happened.

Dad was starting to boil. 'It's that mealy-mouthed Martian, Mr Tugg, isn't it?!' he roared.

'Just come with us, sir,' said one of the policemen. 'It's best if you come quietly. There are some questions you need to answer.' He turned to Mum. 'There's a room where you and the children can wait. If you could please follow us while we escort this gentleman to the holding room.'

So we did. We all trailed behind Dad as he was led away, with everyone in the customs hall watching us until we disappeared. We were settled in the waiting room and another policeman brought us some drinks.

Meanwhile, we could hear the faint drone of

voices from the room next door where Dad was being questioned. It took two hours, two whole boring hours. When Dad came out he was still seething.

'You won't believe this. I have been accused of stealing Elvis.'

Mum's hands flew to her face. 'No!'

'Yes. I have to report to our local police station tomorrow morning, where I shall probably be officially charged. I could be sent to prison.'

'No!' said Mum again.

'Oh yes. And you know who's behind this? Mr Tugg. But, before you say anything, get this – it's not Mr Tugg. At least it's not Mr Tugg our neighbour. It's his cousin, who is also called Mr Tugg and is A FARMER! The farmer who lost a sheep!'

Mum's hand flew to her mouth. 'Oh, Ron, I'm so sorry! I knew there was something I meant to do before we left. You remember I rang round all the farmers, asking them if they'd lost a sheep, and there was one who just wouldn't answer? I was going to get back to him, but with all the excitement of winning the WhoTube competition and going to America and trying to get you unstuck from a million bits of spaghetti I forgot all about it! Oh, it's all my fault. I'm so sorry!'

Mum and Dad stared at each other for several moments until Dad walked across to her, flung his arms round her and gave Mum a huge hug. Then he began laughing. My dad is so weird sometimes! He had just been arrested for sheep stealing and he was laughing!

'It's all completely bonkers!' he cried. 'The whole world is bonkers!'

At last he calmed down and wiped the tears from his eyes. 'Come on, kids, let's get home. I'm dying to have a word with the Martian AND his Martian cousin.'

The car was loaded up with all our luggage and we headed home. Granny and Lancelot were standing at our front door and as soon as Dad got

out of the car Granny began weeping.

'My son,' she sobbed. 'A common criminal!'

'Mother, I am not a common criminal. I'm a
very UN-common criminal and I'll tell you why –
because I'm a criminal that hasn't done anything.
It's all that idiot Martian's fault – him and his
idiot cousin.'

Dad went straight round to Mr Tugg's house and knocked loudly on the front door. Well, that made a change for a start. It was usually Mr Tugg who came round to our house to protest. Now it was Dad doing the complaining.

The door opened and Mr Tugg popped out his bald head and glared at Dad.

'Hah!' snapped Mr Tugg. 'Now the whole world can see what you're really like, you, you sheep robber!'

'And now the whole world can see what YOU'RE really like!' shouted Dad. 'You bone-headed, bumbling, banana-brained, bug-eyed,

bad-tempered, big-mouth, blockheaded, bat-faced, barking bogey-bum! I told you before and I'll tell you again. That sheep of your cousin's followed me home. It's not my fault if it's as stupid as you and your cousin. It followed me home and I have looked after it ever since. What's more, my wife tried to contact your cousin before we went away, but he wasn't answering his phone – probably because he was out being Little Bo Peep looking for his sheep. Tomorrow morning I shall report to the local police station and tell them the truth, the whole truth, and nothing but the truth and you and your cousin will look like the pair of pointless, interfering nobodies you are. Good night!'

Goodness, Dad really was upset. In fact, he had done exactly what Mr Tugg does most of the time. He had erupted like a volcano, thundered like a hurricane and swept Mr Tugg away like a tsunami. By the time Dad got back to our house Mr Tugg was still standing in his doorway, rocking backwards and forwards, wondering what had hit him.

I saw Mrs Tugg go to her husband and take him by the arm. 'Come inside and have a cup of tea, dear. I did warn you. I did say that Ron would never do such a thing.' She pulled Mr Tugg back inside and the front door was closed.

It was great to be back home and since Granny and Lancelot had heard Dad ranting and raving at Mr Tugg they now knew the truth of the matter as well. Actually, I guess the whole street had heard Dad protesting his innocence.

Anyhow, we spent the rest of the day telling Granny and Lancelot about all our adventures in America and soon everything seemed as if it was back to normal. Well, as normal as it ever is in our house.

Lancelot had recorded the news on TV, which showed us meeting the president and his wife and then the launch. It's pretty weird seeing yourself like that, actually on-screen. So now the whole family has been watched by millions, not just Cheese and his famous bottom!

Dad went to the police station the next morning and explained everything very carefully. Mum went with him. The police made a few checks and it was obvious that Dad wasn't making anything up so they tore up the charge sheet and let him go.

Of course Dad made the whole thing into a huge drama that he told his friends and it kept them laughing for about a week. As for poor Mr Tugg, he and his farmer cousin actually came round to the house and apologized. (I thought that was pretty brave and amazing. Mr Tugg must have swallowed an awfully big lump of pride in order to do that.)

Dad accepted the apology with good grace, but he did hand Farmer Tugg an envelope at the same time.

'What's this?' barked Farmer Tugg, opening the envelope and pulling out a single folded sheet of paper.

Bill for Bed and Board for one sheep

Hay and fodder for 7 nights	£40.00
One double room for 7 nights	£70.00
For good care	£40.00
Total:	£150.00

Farmer Tugg read it, glared at my dad, turned purple, began to splutter, suddenly snapped his mouth shut, gritted his teeth, pulled out his cheque book and wrote a cheque for the full amount. Then he grabbed his cousin by the arm and the two of them left.

Dad looked at the cheque in his hand and smiled.

'Come on, everyone,' he said. 'We're all going out to eat tonight. Mr and Mr Tugg have just paid for a lovely dinner! Whoopee!' And he began singing. '*Food, glorious food . . .!*'

'Stop him!' cried Mum. 'Somebody stop him!'

We all crowded round Dad, trying to get a hand over his mouth.

'Help!' cried Dad. 'Someone save me!'

'SILLY DADDY!' shouted Cheese and Tomato.

Jeremy Strong once worked in a bakery, putting the jam into three thousand doughnuts every night. Now he puts the jam in stories instead, which he finds much more exciting. At the age of three, he fell out of a first-floor bedroom window and landed on his head. His mother says that this damaged him for the rest of his life and refuses to take any responsibility. He loves writing stories because he says it is 'the only time you alone have complete control and can make anything happen'. His ambition is to make you laugh (or at least snuffle). Jeremy Strong lives near Bath with his wife, Gillie, three cats and a flying cow.

www.jeremystrong.co.uk